The Old Woman Who Loved to Read

John Winch

Holiday House/New York

In a small farmhouse in the country lived an old woman who loved to read.

She had once lived in the city, but life there was no longer quiet and peaceful, so she decided to move.

In her new home she had many chores, both inside . . .

and out.

In spring she had an unexpected visitor

who was very demanding

and stayed on until summer.

In summer the old woman thought she would have time at
last to read, but the fruit needed harvesting

and had to be preserved for the coming seasons.

The summer was hot and very, very dry.

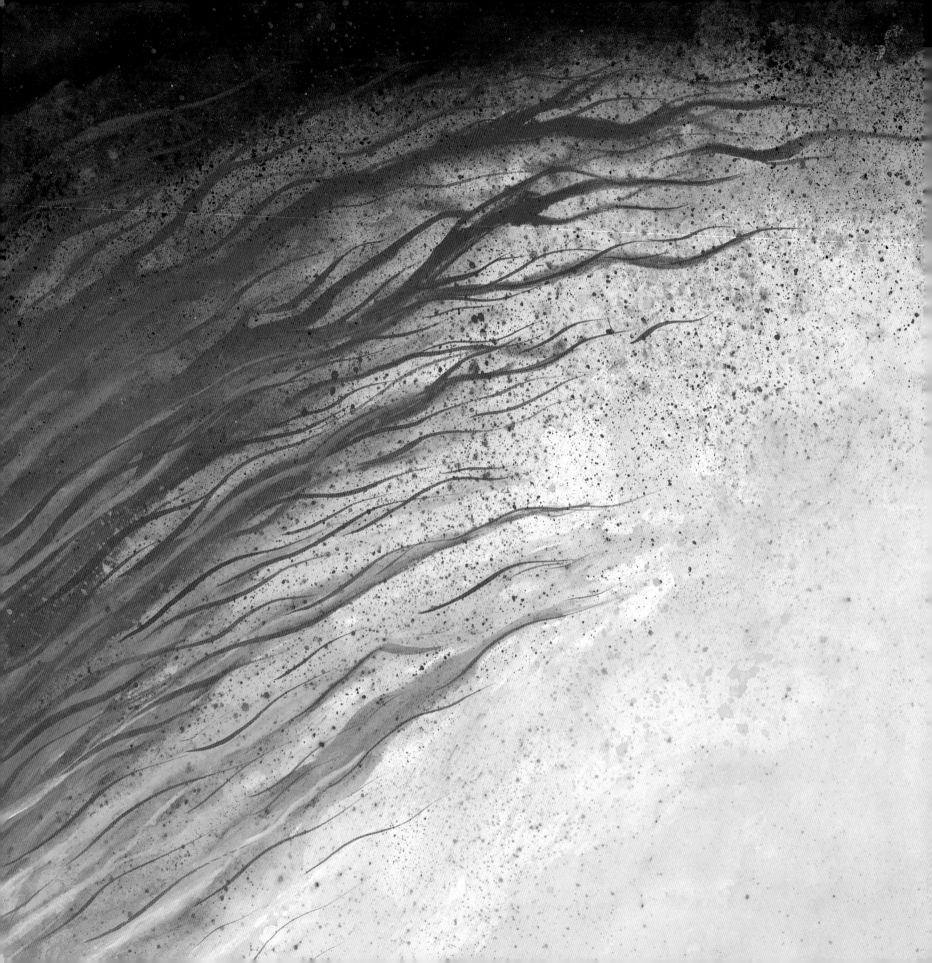

She had intended to read in the autumn but the rains came early

She had intended to read in the autumn but the rains came early and lasted throughout the winter.

But in the heart of winter when she had finished all her tasks, tended the animals and stocked the larder, all was quiet and peaceful

and the old woman
could enjoy her reading.